P9-DDV-485

THE DAY
I HAD TO PLAY WITH
MY SISTER

THE DAY
I HAD TO PLAY WITH
MY SISTER

An Early I CAN READ Book

by CROSBY BONSALL

Harper & Row, Publishers
New York, Evanston, San Francisco, London

for Laura

6-14

Want to play a game?

You hide.

I will find you.

Okay?

One.

Two.

Three.

Here

I

come,

ready

or not.

THAT IS NOT THE WAY
TO PLAY THE GAME!

You HIDE, okay?

Hide in back of a tree.

Or hide here, see?

And I will find you. Okay?

One. Two. Three.

Here I come,

ready or not.

I know where you are.

I know. Here!

No, here!

No.

Well, I know

where you are.

You are

in the doghouse.

Now, you cut that out!

Hear?

This time I will hide.

You look for me, okay?

You say

one, two, three.

You say

here I come,

ready or not.

Okay?

Never mind.

I will hide.

You just look for me.

Now don't forget

to look

for me.

GET OFF MY LAP!

I don't want

to play with you

anymore.